ABC Warriors

ATOMIC ★ BACTERIAL ★ CHEMICAL

THE VOLGAN WAR

VOLUME 02

ABC WARRIORS CREATED BY PAT MILLS, KEVIN O'NEILL, MIKE MCMAHON AND BRENDAN MCCARTHY

THE POINT OF NO RETURN

When the ABC Warriors were first created, they were pure science fiction and the future in which they were set was a very long way away. But today we are fast catching up. Consider, for instance, the indestructibility of the ABC Warriors whose computer brains have survived endless conflicts through several millennia. Scientists are already warning that many of the new computer viruses defy extermination reaching what one expert has called "the cockroach stage".

There is also the danger of unleashing homicidal robots like Blackblood into the world. Another artificial intelligence expert has warned, "We're rapidly reaching the time when new robots should undergo tests, similar to ethical and clinical trials for new drugs, before they can be introduced."

There are unmanned flying predator robots who can seek out and kill humans with the precise and deadly accuracy of Joe Pineapples. In Korea, Samsung have autonomous sentry robots with a "shoot to kill" capability comparable to the Mark One version of Hammerstein. And Japanese robots from Mitsubishi can "learn" their owner's behaviour and recharge themselves so they are continually working. I wonder how long before a robot starts learning the arcane knowledge that Deadlock absorbed in his long years of studying magic.

Then there is Mongrol who has formed an emotional bond with his creator Lara. Whether it is real or simulated, it is not dissimilar to "nursebots" currently being developed who simulate empathy with their patients. Zippo is a master of disguise and there are now intelligent viruses that copy people's voices and are used by criminals to bypass speech recognition systems and impersonate people on line.

Vehicles now have the ability to park themselves and use GPS to apply brakes at stop signs. These are the kind of limited controls that would be needed for a more basic robot like Mek-Quake, but there would always be the fear that – through a virus or a technical error - such a robot bulldozer could still run amok. The U.S. Army has funded an intelligent robot forklift truck for war zones that recognizes voice commands and can move independently. Whether it also says, "Big Jobs" is unknown.

The incentive for the Pentagon to manufacture intelligent war machines is that human troops can be used in secondary waves after robots have carried out the brunt of the fighting. Consequently, there will be far less humans going home in flag-draped coffins. However, there would be no such military funerals for intelligent machines like the ABC Warriors; after all, as Howard Quartz, the manufacturer of the ABC Warriors, has said, "No one mourns a robot."

A robot called the PackBot is used in Iraq to locate and blow up enemy bombs, also blowing itself up in the process at a cost of $150,000 per robot. It can only be a matter of time before indestructible machines like Hammerstein will carry out these same tasks. A Pentagon spokesman has stated, "Robots don't get hungry. "They're not afraid. They don't forget their orders. They don't care if the guy next to them has just been shot. Will they do a better job than humans? Yes." That sounds very much like the ABC Warriors.

The singularity, the point of no return, could well be soon. This is the time when robots become so intelligent, they are able to build ever more intelligent and powerful versions of themselves without reference to humans. When that moment arrives, the Warriors adventures may be seen as closer to science fact than science fiction and the truth may be even stranger than the fiction depicted in this second volume of *The Volgan Wars*.

Pat Mills, **October 2009**

DEDICATIONS

For Lisa

For Anja, Bayon, Thai and Nepali

SAVAGE - BOOK 5 (1984)

2009. Mark One War Droids are used by Howard Quartz's Robusters group to help liberate Britain from the Volgan invaders. But the Mark One lacks the ability to correctly identify friend from foe and several massacres of civilians follow.

ROBUSTERS - YESTERDAY'S HERO

The Mark Three War Droid prototype – Hammerstein – is deployed alongside US soldiers to help liberate Europe from the Volgans. Programmed with complex emotions and able to make moral judgements, Hammerstein is an outstanding military success.

ABC WARRIORS - THE MEKNIFICENT SEVEN

Robots have now replaced humans in combat. They are known as the A.B.C. Warriors; resistant to Atomic, Bacterial and Chemical warfare. Hammerstein and six other Warriors play key roles in the destruction of the Volgan Empire. "The Meknificent Seven" are then sent to Mars to bring peace to the Red Planet by resolving conflicts between the settlers and warring trans-planetary corporations.

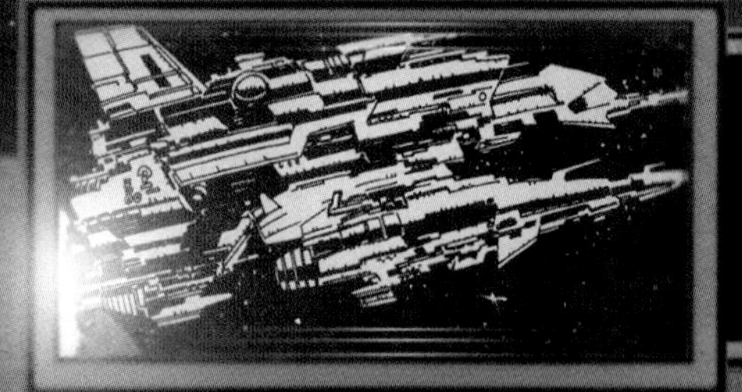

ABC WARRIORS - THE UNTOLD STORY (1). RETURN TO EARTH

The ABC Warriors split up and Hammerstein returns to Earth. He now wears a different head unit, but retains his original humanoid head. Under unknown circumstances, he ends up for sale in a used robot showroom where he meets the garbage robot Ro-Jaws.

RO-BUSTERS

2078. Howard Quartz now has a robot body, but retains his human brain, and is known as Mr. Ten Per Cent. He buys Ro-Jaws and Hammerstein for his Robusters disaster squad which includes the demolition robot Mek-Quake. Mek-Quake also features in The Terra Meks where a squad of giant robots are sent to destroy a city.

THE FALL AND RISE OF RO-JAWS AND HAMMERSTEIN

Ro-Jaws and Hammerstein lead a robot escape from Earth to a robot refuge moon orbiting Saturn. But Ro-Jaws and Hammerstein have to remain behind on Earth.

NEMESIS - BOOK 3

Mek-Quake – in a giant humanoid body – fights for the human Terminators against Aliens led by Nemesis the Warlock.

NEMESIS - BOOK 4. THE GOTHIC EMPIRE
Ro-Jaws is working at a hotel on planet Britannia in the alien Gothic Empire. He meets the alien Warlock Nemesis and becomes his personal assistant. Subsequently Nemesis recruits most of the original ABC Warriors to defend the Gothic Empire. The Warriors remain with Nemesis in a further adventure set at the End of the World.

ABC WARRIORS - THE BLACK HOLE BYPASS
The Warriors are sent by Nemesis to the Blackhole Bypass to prevent the End of Time.

ABC WARRIORS - THE KHRONICLES OF KHAOS
Led by Deadlock, the Warriors follow the path of Khaos in a series of adventures.

DEADLOCK - RETURN TO TERMIGHT
Deadlock helps an alien biker gang in Termight in the years following the deaths of Nemesis and Torquemada.

ABC WARRIORS - THE UNTOLD STORY (2)
Mystery surrounds the circumstances under which the Warriors return to Mars.

ABC WARRIORS - THE THIRD ELEMENT (RETURN TO MARS)
Mars has a dormant planetary consciousness known as Medusa. Under the impact of terra-forming, Medusa awakes and fights back against the human settlers. Arriving on Mars, the ABC Warriors try to restore the balance between the colonists and the hostile world they have settled on.

ABC WARRIORS - THE SHADOW WARRIORS
A civil war breaks out on Mars between the humans who have adapted to Medusa and those who would try to destroy her. The ABC Warriors 'increase the peace' but have to deal with a group of robot mercenaries sent to destroy them.

ABC WARRIORS - THE VOLGAN WARS VOLUME 01
After leaving Mek-Quake in a robot asylum, the Warriors travel to Marineris City to rescue a comrade who will replace him. En-route, they recall their adventures in the Volgan War and their greatest enemy - Volkhan. They are unaware that Volkhan is now a prisoner in the same asylum and is planning his escape.

THE VOLGAN WAR

Script: Pat Mills
Art: Clint Langley
Letters: Simon Bowland

Originally published in *2000 AD* Progs 1550-1559

BROADBAND ASYLUM, MARS.
I DON'T KNOW WHY WE BOTHER. VOLKHAN'S WATCHED AND LISTENED TO TWENTY-FOUR-SEVEN.
THERE'S NO WAY HE'S GETTING OUT OF THERE.

ANYWAY, HE'S A **WRECK**, A SHADOW OF HIS FORMER SELF.
EVEN SO-- JUST IMAGINE IF HE EVER ***DID*** ESCAPE...

HELP
HELP ME
NO PROBLEMS, MEK-QUAKE?
NO. ALL DONE.
ALL RIGHT. YOU CAN RETURN TO THE DAY ROOM.

AN INCOMING HOLOGRAM CALL...WHO COULD THAT BE?
BLACKBLOOD!
THERE'S SOMETHING I HAVE TO TELL YOU, MEK-QUAKE.
THE WARRIORS ARE COMING TO COLLECT ME? MEK-QUAKE IS BACK ON THE TEAM?
NO. YOU'RE BEING REPLACED BY A NEW ROBOT.
DO I-- HGRRHH!-- KNOW THIS ROBOT?
I DON'T THINK SO. HIS NAME IS ZIPPO. WE'RE ON OUR WAY TO MARINERIS CITY TO FIND HIM NOW.
IT WON'T LAST, YOU KNOW!
IT NEVER DOES! THE NEW A.B.C. WARRIORS NEVER STAY!
IT'S A MISTAKE THEY'VE JUST GOT TO MAKE, MEK-QUAKE.
I JUST THOUGHT I SHOULD TELL YOU...AS A FRIEND.
WHY ARE YOU BACK HERE, MEK-QUAKE?
I THOUGHT YOU'D CLEANED VOLKHAN'S CELL?
I JUST REMEMBERED...
...THERE'S A BIT I MISSED.

THE GREAT SAND OCEAN.

A LOT OF THE WAY WE ARE IS SURVIVORS' GUILT. WE'RE HOME. WE'RE OKAY.
BUT MOST WARRIORS DIDN'T MAKE IT.
"WE'RE NOT GOING TO MAKE THE VOLGAN REPUBLIC SAFE FOR DEMOCRACY," I TOLD MY BOYS. "WE ARE HERE FOR ONE REASON ALONE: OIL."
"BUT WE'RE STILL GOING TO FIGHT, BECAUSE THAT'S HOW WE'RE PROGRAMMED."

THE HARDEST THING WHEN I GOT BACK WAS HUMANS SLAPPING ME ON THE BACK AND SAYING, "GREAT JOB, STEELHORN!"
THEY WANTED IT TO BE A GOOD WAR SO THEY COULD SLEEP AT NIGHT.
BUT WE KNOW IT WASN'T A GOOD WAR. THERE'S NO SUCH THING AS A GOOD WAR.
YOU WERE SOLDIERS. YOU SHOULD BE PROUD OF COMPLETING YOUR KILL QUOTAS AND SURVIVING.
AS YOU ARE? YOU SEEM VERY PLEASED WITH YOURSELF FOR SOME REASON...
PERHAPS YOU WOULD LIKE TO HEAR MY RECOLLECTION OF MY ADVENTURES WITH MY STRAW DOGS BEFORE I WAS REPROGRAMMED? SSSS!
LISTEN TO HIM. JUST THE THOUGHT OF IT IS BRINGING BACK HIS OLD SPEECH PROGRAM.
I'M GOING UP TO THE BRIDGE. I DON'T WANT TO HEAR ABOUT HOW MANY OF MY BOYS HE KILLED.
STOP THIS SENTIMENTAL FOOLISHNESS. THEY WERE NOT YOUR "BOYS".
THEY WERE MASS-PRODUCED WAR MACHINES, WHOSE ONLY FUNCTION WAS TO FIGHT AND DIE.
THEY WERE HEROES.

VLADIVOSTOCK, 2081.
YOU ARE SURROUNDED, HAMMERSTEINSSSSS!
LAY DOWN YOUR ARMS AND YOU HAVE MY WORD YOU WILL BE TREATED AS PRISONERS OF WAR! SSSSS!
WHAT DOES HE MEAN, "TREATED AS PRISONERS OF WAR"?
HE MEANS WE'LL BE SMELTED DOWN AND TURNED INTO AK47S.
THERE'S NO GENEVA CONVENTION FOR ROBOTS.
PITY OUR MANUFACTURER NEVER TRUSTED US WITH A SELF-DESTRUCT MECHANISM.
THAT'S iQUARTZ ROBOTICS FOR YOU.
MAYBE WE CAN TAKE OUT SOME OF THE EYEPODS FIRST.

COULD YOU IMAGINE HOWARD QUARTZ PERMITTING US TO DESTROY OURSELVES? RISKING HIS PRECIOUS PROFITS?
LET'S USE UP THE LAST OF OUR TORCS--
--AND GO OUT FIGHTING!

BLAM! BLAM! BLAM! BLAM! BLAM! BLAM! BLAM! BLAM! BLAM! BLAM!
STOP!
I WON'T SEE ANYMORE OF THESE SENSELESS SUICIDE CHARGES!
IF *YOU* SURRENDER, BLACKBLOOD MAY SPARE *OUR* LIVES.
I KNOW THE GENEVA CONVENTION DOESN'T APPLY TO YOU HAMMERSTEINS, BUT IT STILL APPLIES TO HUMANS.
YOU THINK HE CAN BE TRUSTED, COLONEL?
PROBABLY NOT. BUT IT'S GOT TO BE WORTH A TRY. THERE ARE INNOCENT CIVILIANS TO THINK OF.
IN THAT CASE WE'LL BE HAPPY TO DO SO. SAVING HUMANS IS ONE OF OUR PRIMARY DIRECTIVES.
I'M SORRY HE WON'T SPARE YOU AS WELL. HAMMERSTEINS ARE THE BEST COMBAT MACHINES IN THE ARMY. COURAGEOUS... CARING... INTELLIGENT...
IT WAS A PRIVILEGE TO FIGHT WITH YOU.
THANK YOU, COLONEL.
HOLD YOUR FIRE, BLACKBLOOD! WE'RE COMING OUT!

AT LAST! MY PATIENCE WAS EXHAUSTED! *SSSS!*
LAY DOWN YOUR ARMS, A.B.C. WARRIORS!
KA-CHING!
KA-CHING!
KA-CHING!
KA-CHING!
KA-CHING!
KA-CHING!
KA-CHING!
KA-CHING!
SEE YOU IN A NEW CYCLE, BROTHER.
YES. WE CAN DIE KNOWING WE WERE COST-EFFECTIVE. WE DESTROYED MANY ENEMY ROBOTS AND SAVED HUMAN LIVES.
OUR ***PROTOTYPE*** WOULD BE PROUD OF US.

FIRE!
HAMMERSTEINS! THEY COST ME TOO MANY OF MY DOGSSSSS!

SSSSSSSSS!
SSSSSSSSS!

BLAM!
AAARRGH!!

REPLACEMENTS HAVE ARRIVED FROM THE FACTORY AND ARE ASSEMBLING THEMSELVES, GENERAL.
EXCELLENT.
AND WE HAVE HUMAN PRISONERS FOR YOUR INTERROGATION.
MY CUP RUNNETH OVER! SSSS!
THIS IS COLONEL LEYTON. WE FOUND THESE OBJECTS IN HIS POCKETS.
I WOULD REMIND YOU, GENERAL--HUMANS ARE PROTECTED BY THE CONVENTION.
THIS IS TRUE, COLONEL--APART FROM THOSE WHO WEAR THE BADGE OF THE SPECIAL FORCES, RESPONSIBLE FOR SABOTAGE AND TERRORISM.
LIKE YOURSELF! SSSSS!
LEYTON
AN INTERESTING LIGHTER, COLONEL... SSSS!
THOUGH I WALK THROUGH THE VALLEY OF THE SHADOW OF DEATH I WILL FEAR NO EVIL FOR I AM THE EVILLEST
"THOUGH I WALK THROUGH THE VALLEY OF THE SHADOW OF DEATH I WILL FEAR NO EVIL FOR I AM THE EVILLEST SON OF A BITCH IN THE VALLEY."
IT WAS A PRESENT FROM ONE OF MY ROBOTS.
BUT SURELY I AM "THE EVILLEST SON OF A BITCH IN THE VALLEY"?
THEN YOU'D BETTER TAKE IT, GENERAL.
KA-CHINQ
THANK YOU VERY MUCH.

SO WHAT ELSE HAVE WE HERE?
YOUR DIARY...
"THIS TERRIBLE WAR IS A SET-UP TO STEAL THE VOLGANS' OIL AND MAKE MONEY FOR ROBOT WEAPONS MANUFACTURERS LIKE HOWARD QUARTZ."
"THE GENERAL PUBLIC SHOULD BE TOLD WHAT IS REALLY GOING ON."
WHO IS GENERAL PUBLIC?
THAT'S JUST A FIGURE OF SPEECH. YOU MUSTN'T TAKE IT LITERALLY.
OF COURSE I AM AWARE IT IS A CODE NAME, COLONEL.
BUT WHAT IS THE GENERAL'S REAL NAME?
NO, IT'S ONLY AN EXPRESSION. THERE IS NO "GENERAL PUBLIC".
DON'T GET SMART WITH ME, COLONEL.
I HAVE WAYS OF MAKING YOU REVEAL HIS TRUE IDENTITY...SSSS!
THIS IS HILARIOUS!
HE DOES NOT EXIST, BLACKBLOOD! EXCEPT IN YOUR IMAGINATION!
YOU THINK YOU CAN BLUFF YOUR WAY OUT OF TROUBLE BY TURNING GENERAL PUBLIC INTO A JOKE?
BLAM!
WELL, LAUGH THIS OFF! SSSS!
DAMN! NOW I SHALL NEVER KNOW WHO GENERAL PUBLIC IS...

LORD VOLKHAN IS ON THE HOLO-VID FOR YOU, GENERAL.
VERY WELL.
MY IKON!
EXCELLENT WORK, GENERAL. YOU HAVE DESTROYED THE A.B.C. CRIMINALS. VLADIVOSTOCK IS IN OUR HANDS ONCE MORE.
BUT A GROUP OF WOUNDED OFFICERS ARE ATTEMPTING TO ESCAPE TO THE NORTH, ASSISTED BY B.E.A.R.S.: "BATTLEFIELD EXTRACTION AND RETRIEVAL ROBOTS".
MAKE SURE THEY FAIL!
HURRY UP AND ASSEMBLE YOURSELVES! THIS WILL BE A CHANCE FOR YOU TO BE BLOODED IN BATTLE! SSSSS!
ONLY ANOTHER TWO CLICKS TO THE DOCKS, SIR. THERE'S A HIGH-SPEED CRAFT WAITING TO TAKE YOU OFF.
I'VE JUST HEARD COLONEL LEYTON WAS KILLED, ZIPPO. SHOT BY BLACKBLOOD.
HUGG BEAR

I'M SORRY TO HEAR THAT, SIR. COLONEL LEYTON WAS THE BEST OFFICER I'VE FOUGHT UNDER--
EYEPODS!
IT'S BLACKBLOOD!
PAYBACK TIME!
B.E.A.R
B.E.A.R

ABC

"Delete dirty thoughts"
Urgent
INBOX THOUGHT MAIL
DOWNLOADING NOW ...
Reply
Virus Warning
Delete

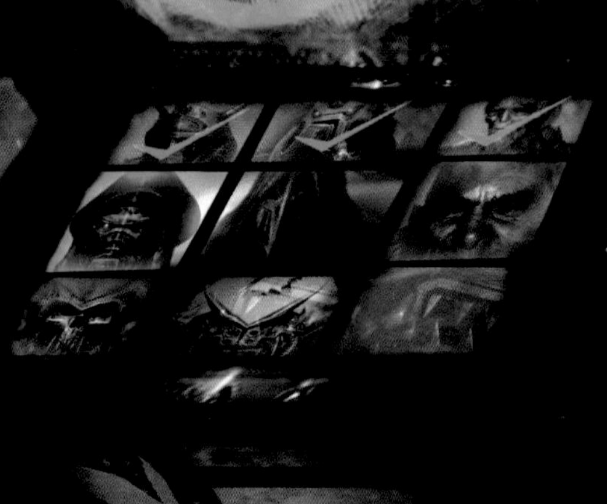

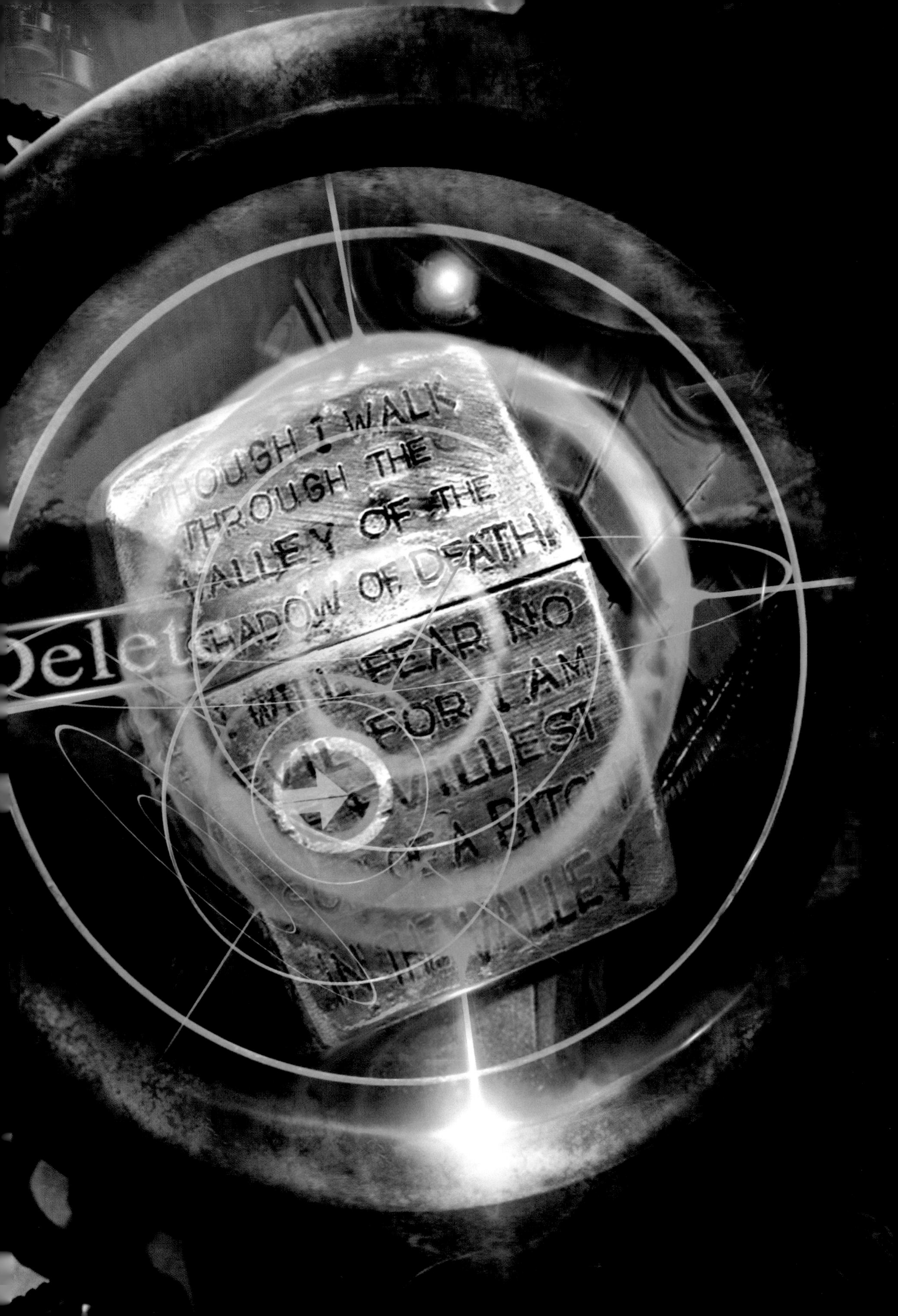
THOUGH I WALK
THROUGH THE
VALLEY OF THE
SHADOW OF DEATH
FEAR NO
FOR I AM

THERE'S A CHIP IN THE LIGHTER I GAVE COLONEL LEYTON, SO I COULD RENDEZVOUS WITH HIM...
...MY SENSORS TELL ME *BLACKBLOOD* HAS IT NOW.
I'VE ALIGNED IT TO THE TARGET RECOGNITION SYSTEM IN THE MISSILE.

NATURALLY MY COLLISSION AVOIDANCE SENSORS ARE STATE OF THE ART! SSSS!
NOW DESTROY THEM! TAKE NO PRISONERSSSSS! VOLKHAN HIMSELF HAS ORDERED IT!
NONE MUST LEAVE VLADIVOSTOK ALIVE! SSSSS!
BEAT! BEAT! AND--
WHAT...?
WHAT'S THE MATTER WITH THEM? IDENTIFYING AND ATTACKING THE CORRECT ENEMY IS BASIC ROBOT PROGRAMMING!
SSSSABOTAGE!

THIS IS A LUCKY BREAK! WE'RE GONNA MAKE IT! ARE YOU SPECIAL OPS GUYS RESPONSIBLE, ZIPPO?
NO. I'M AS BAFFLED AS YOU ARE...
...BUT THIS IS MY CHANCE TO KILL BLACKBLOOD!
NO. YOUR MISSION COMES FIRST.
GET THE OFFICERS TO SAFETY.
BY WHOSE AUTHORITY, SIR?
MY NAME IS COLONEL LASH.
I AM YOUR NEW COMMANDING OFFICER, AGENT ORANGE.

VOLKHAN WISHES TO SPEAK TO YOU URGENTLY, GENERAL.

DO YOU HAVE ANY EXPLANATION FOR THE MALFUNCTION OF YOUR AK49S, GENERAL?

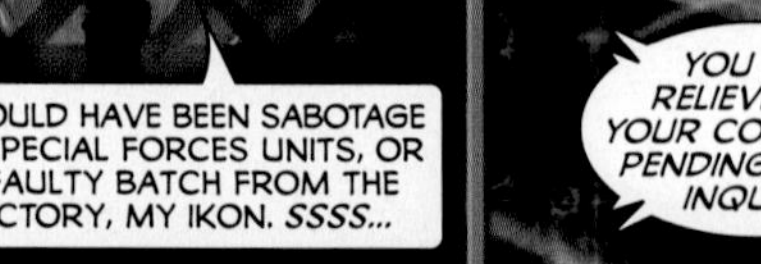
IT COULD HAVE BEEN SABOTAGE BY SPECIAL FORCES UNITS, OR A FAULTY BATCH FROM THE FACTORY, MY IKON. SSSS...

YOU ARE RELIEVED OF YOUR COMMAND, PENDING A FULL INQUIRY.
AND SHOULD IT FIND YOU GUILTY OF CRIMINAL NEGLIGENCE, YOU KNOW WHAT TO EXPECT...

IZHEVSK ROBOTICS FACTORY.
THE WAR ROBOTS BUILT HERE ARE RENOWNED FOR THEIR RELIABILITY, PERFECT ENGINEERING AND DESIGN, GENERAL.
I KNOW, DIRECTOR. I WAS MANUFACTURED HERE MYSELF. SSSS!
THEY ARE SUPERIOR IN EVERY WAY TO THE CRIMINAL ROBOTS PRODUCED BY IQUARTZ ROBOTICS.
SO WHAT WENT WRONG?
IT IS PUZZLING. BEFORE THEY LEAVE THE FACTORY, ROBOTS ARE COMBAT-TESTED BY ATTACKING A.B.C. PRISONERS...
...SO THERE SHOULD BE NO PROBLEM WITH THEM IDENTIFYING THE ENEMY.
LET'S TALK TO THEIR DESIGNERS: MIKHAIL AND MARINA ZHIGUNOV.
THEY HAVE BEEN HONOURED WITH MANY AWARDS FOR THEIR SERVICES TO THE COUNTRY...
...INCLUDING "THE ORDER OF KRASNODON" AND THE VASHKOV PRIZE FOR DISTINGUISHED SERVICES TO THE MOTHERLAND.
WE WERE SORRY TO HEAR ABOUT THE PROBLEMS WITH YOUR AK49S, GENERAL...
CORRECTION. YOUR AK49SSSSS.

ALL OUR ROBOTS ARE MONITORED FOR VIRUSES BEFORE BEING SENT TO THE FRONT.
IF THERE WERE A VIRUS IN YOUR *"STRAW DOGS"*, IT WOULD HAVE BEEN DETECTED.
I SUSPECT THEY SUCCUMBED TO A NEW ENEMY VIRUS IN THE FIELD.
IT SEEMS UNLIKELY. EARLIER BATCHES PERFORMED PERFECTLY. *SSSS...*

LIKE I SAID, GENERAL--A ***NEW*** VIRUS...

MUM! WE'RE GOING TO BE LATE!

PLEASE EXCUSE ME, GENERAL. I'VE PROMISED TO TAKE MY DAUGHTER TO THE CONCERT.

LARA, THIS IS GENERAL BLACKBLOOD.

HELLO.

SSSO, ARE YOU PLANNING TO FOLLOW YOUR DISTINGUISHED PARENTS AND BECOME A ROBOT DESIGNER, LARA?

MAYBE, GENERAL. IF THE WORLD HASN'T BEEN BLOWN UP BY THEN.

DAD, ARE YOU ***SURE*** YOU CAN'T COME?

I'M SORRY, LARA. I MUST FINISH THESE REPORTS. BUT YOU HAVE A GREAT TIME.

DON'T WORK ***TOO*** LATE, MIKHAIL.

YES. YOU SHOULDN'T WORK ***TOO*** LATE, MIKHAIL.

PRELIMINARY VOICE ANALYSIS INDICATES THE ZHIGUNOVS ARE ***LYING*** AND HAVE BEEN ***SABOTAGING*** THEIR OWN CREATIONS.

AND I ***KNOW*** HOW TO DISCOVER THE ***TRUTH...***

IZHEVSK SECRET POLICE HEADQUARTERS.
I AM ALREADY AWARE YOU ARE HAVING AN AFFAIR WITH ZHIGUNOV, OLGA.
THAT IS NOT AGAINST THE LAW, GENERAL.
BUT HELPING THE ENEMY ISSSSS!
HOW DO THEY SABOTAGE THE ROBOTS?
I DON'T KNOW, GENERAL.
YOU WOULD DO WELL TO TELL ME THE TRUTH...
THEY HAVE A DACHA DEEP IN THE FOREST. MIKHAIL TOOK ME THERE ONCE.
THERE'S A LABORATORY UNDERNEATH. IT'S WHERE THEY WORK ON VIRUSES THAT ARE UNDETECTABLE BY THE SCANNERS.
THANK YOU.
AAAHRGH!

IT'S GETTING DARK. LARA SHOULD BE HERE BY NOW.
OH, YOU KNOW WHAT IT'S LIKE WHEN SHE'S WITH NIKOLAY. SHE LOSES ALL TRACK OF TIME.
YOU DON'T THINK THOSE TWO ARE...YOU KNOW...?
NO. THEY'RE JUST FRIENDS.
SHE'S FASCINATED BY HIS STRANGE WAYS...
WELL, THIS NEW VIRUS SHOULD SCREW UP ANOTHER REGIMENT OF AK49S.
IT'S THE ONLY WAY TO STOP THIS CRAZY WAR.
IS IT, MIKHAIL? SOMETIMES I THINK THE GENERAL PUBLIC DOESN'T CARE.
GENERAL PUBLIC! I KNEW HE WAS BEHIND THIS!

NO ONE CARES AS LONG AS ROBOTS AND NOT HUMANS ARE DYING.
GOOD EVENING.
I SSSHALL WAIT UNTIL YOU ARE JOINED BY LARA.
THEN YOU WILL TELL ME WHAT I NEED TO KNOW.
IN PARTICULAR, THE IDENTITY OF YOUR LEADER-- GENERAL PUBLIC.
AND WHO IS THIS NIKOLAY LARA IS VISITING?
HE'S AN OLD BELIEVER. THEY HAVE A SETTLEMENT NEARBY.
AH, YESSSS. A BREAKAWAY RELIGIOUS MOVEMENT FROM THE SEVENTEENTH CENTURY. TO ESCAPE PERSECUTION, THEY DISAPPEARED INTO THE FOREST. SSSSS!

I HEAR LARA RETURNING...!
DO NOT ATTEMPT TO ALERT HER. ACT NORMALLY. WHAT WOULD YOU DO? SSSS!
I DON'T KNOW...ER, SING...?
YES. YES. THAT'S RIGHT...WE'D SING.
THEN SING IF YOU VALUE YOUR LIVESSS!
WIND BREATHE ON HER FACE AND TELL HER IT'S FROM ME...
SSSSING! LOUDER!
GO WIND TO UKRAINE WHERE I LEFT MY LOVE!
LOUDER!
WIND BREATHE ON HER HAIR...
WHAT'S THE MATTER WITH THEM? WHY ARE THEY SINGING LIKE THAT? SOMETHING'S WRONG!

CARESS HER LIPS, STROKE HER EYES...
THEY'RE WARNING ME! IT'S A *TRAP!*
GO WIND TO UKRAINE!
SSSHUT UP!

SSSHUT UP!
BLAM!
SSSHUT UP!
BLAM!
YOU THINK YOU CAN MAKE A FOOL OUT OF BLACKBLOOD!
YOU CAN'T ESSSCAPE ME, LARA. I HAVE THE MOST SOPHISTICATED *DETECTION* SYSTEMS. *SSSSS!*

I KNOW YOU ARE NEAR, LARA. I CAN HEAR YOUR *BREATHING...*
SSSENSE YOUR BODY HEAT...
YOUR *SSSCENT...*
YOU'RE STARTING TO MAKE ME ANGRY, LARA.
FRAG YOU, BLACKBLOOD!
AAAHHHH!
YOU'LL PAY FOR THIS,
LAAARAAAH!

YOU'LL SUFFER FOR THIS, LAAARAAAAH!
NO, BLACKBLOOD. *YOU'LL* SUFFER.
IS IT ONE OF THE CZAR'S SOLDIERS?
IT'S A ROBOT. A WAR MACHINE.
I THINK IT MAY HAVE KILLED MUM AND DAD.
WE COULD CHAIN IT BETWEEN TWO HORSES AND RIP IT APART?
NO, NIKOLAY. IT'S DESIGNED TO FIGHT ATOMIC, BACTERIAL AND CHEMICAL WARS.
WE HAVE TO FIND ANOTHER WAY. HOLD IT DOWN.
OUR MUSKET BALLS DON'T EVEN DENT IT!

NIKOLAY-- BRING ME SOME GUNPOWDER.
YURI-- FORCE ITS MOUTH OPEN.
ITS DESIGNERS NEVER THOUGHT ABOUT GUNPOWDER.
HOW DO YOU KNOW?
BECAUSE MY PARENTS BUILT ROBOTS LIKE THIS.
NO! YOU EVIL WITCH!
THIS IS FOR THEM.

DUMP IT IN THE SWAMP.

WON'T THE CZAR SEND A SEARCH PARTY?
YES, BUT THE TREES WILL INTERFERE WITH ITS SATELLITE SIGNAL. THEY WON'T BE ABLE TO HOME IN ON IT.

IF IT IS STILL ALIVE, IT WILL TAKE IT MONTHS--MAYBE *YEARS*--TO GET OUT OF THERE.

MONSTER!

BEFORE I DIE...THERE'S ONE THING I ***HAVE*** TO KNOW...
WHO... WHO ISSS ***GENERAL PUBLIC?***
YOU'LL NEVER KNOW.
YOU CAN'T STAY HERE NOW, LARA. COME WITH US--WE'LL GO EVEN DEEPER INTO THE FOREST. SOMEWHERE THE CZAR'S MEN WILL NEVER FIND US.
NO, NIKOLAY. I HAVE TO GET AWAY. I'VE AN AUNT IN VILNIUS WHO WILL TAKE ME IN.
I WILL BE SAFE THERE...

THE GREAT SAND OCEAN.
WHAT ARE YOU ALL LOOKING AT ME LIKE THAT FOR?
I THINK YOU'LL AGREE I WAS LUCKY TO SURVIVE. FORTUNATELY, THE SEARCH PARTY FOUND ME AFTER ONLY THREE MONTHS IN THE SWAMP.
YOU MURDERED LARA'S PARENTS?
IT WAS THEM OR ME.
VOLKHAN AWARDED ME THE ORDER OF KRASNODON FOR DISCOVERING THE SABOTEURS.
AND LOOK ON THE BRIGHT SIDE...AT LEAST I MISSED LARA.
CIGAR?
NOW DON'T START ALL THAT TEDIOUS SMUSHING! I'VE JUST HAD A REFIT!
WHEN I'VE FINISHED WITH YOU, EVEN TUBAL CAIN WON'T BE ABLE TO PUT YOU BACK TOGETHER!

IT WAS WARTIME! THEY COMMITTED *TREASON!*
WHAT DID YOU EXPECT ME TO DO, YOU *WUSS?*
TAKE IT EASY, MONGROL. HE'S NOT THE *SAME* BLACKBLOOD NOW. HE WAS REPROGRAMMED.
THAT'S RIGHT! I'VE BEEN REPROGRAMMED! *SSSSS!*
CAN WE PUT THIS ON HOLD FOR NOW?
WE'LL BE DOCKING SHORTLY IN MARINERIS...
OKAY. IT'S NOT IN MY PROGRAMMING TO WALK OUT IN THE MIDDLE OF A MISSION. WE NEED TO RESCUE ZIPPO.
BUT AFTERWARDS I'M NOT PREPARED TO WORK WITH BLACKBLOOD ANY MORE.
WHEN THIS MISSION IS OVER, HE *LEAVES* THE A.B.C. WARRIORS.
OR I DO!

BROADBAND ASYLUM.
GOOD WORK, MEK-QUAKE.
HE IS WAITING FOR YOU.
YOU'VE SWITCHED THE CCTV FOOTAGE?
YEHHHH. AND BROUGHT HIS LIMBS.
IS EVERYTHING ALL RIGHT?
YES, NURSE RATCHET.
JUST ANOTHER QUIET NIGHT...

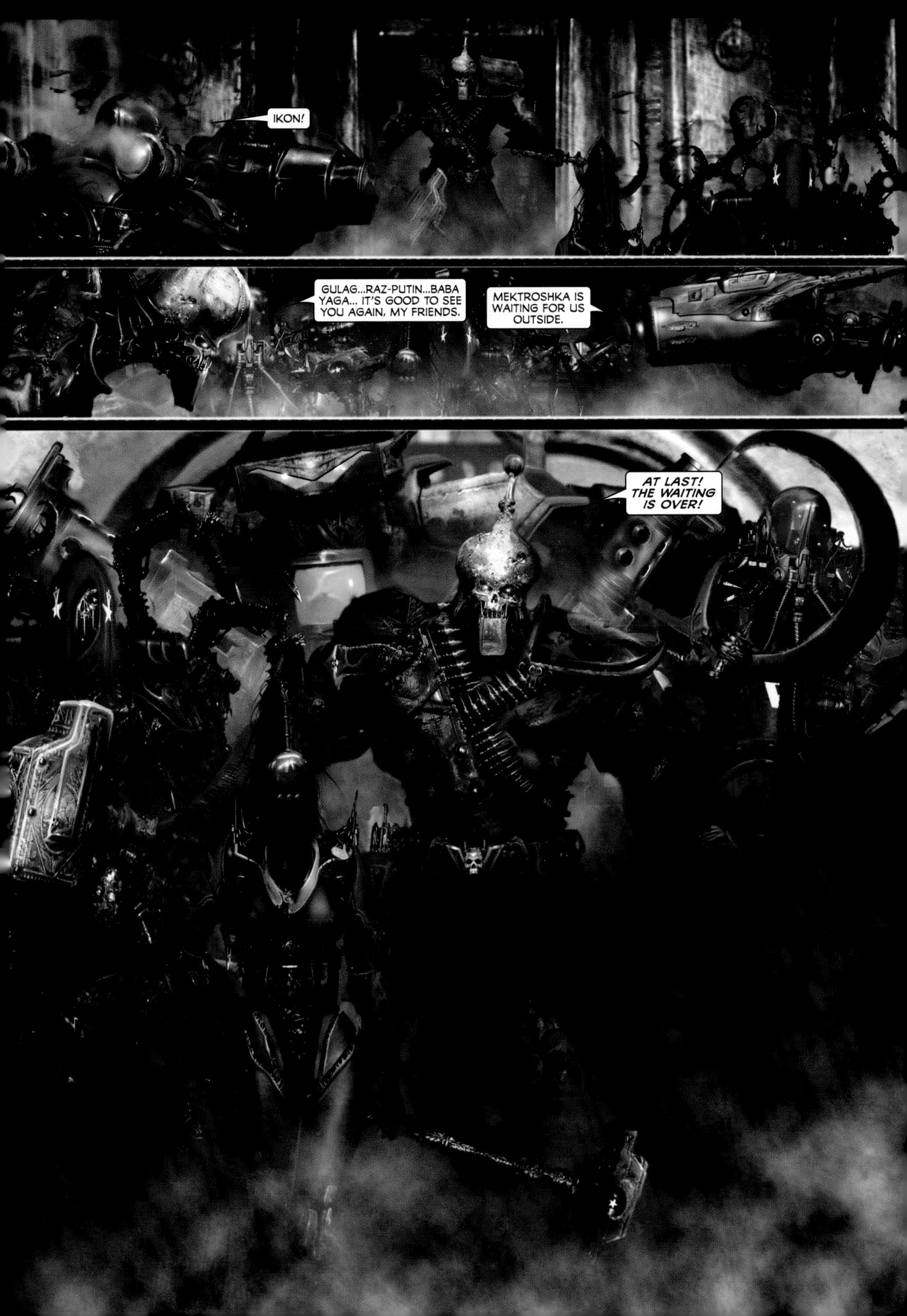
IKON!
GULAG...RAZ-PUTIN...BABA YAGA... IT'S GOOD TO SEE YOU AGAIN, MY FRIENDS.
MEKTROSHKA IS WAITING FOR US OUTSIDE.
AT LAST! THE WAITING IS OVER!

MARINERIS CITY.
WHAT ABOUT PASSPORT AND SECURITY CONTROLS?
STEELHORN'S TAKING CARE OF IT.
HE'S GIVEN US IDENTITIES AS OFF-WORLD DIPLOMATS SO WE DON'T HAVE TO GO THROUGH SECURITY.
WHILE WE ARE AWAITING HIS RETURN, I SHALL TELL *MY* STORY OF THE VOLGAN WAR...

JUST AS WELL-- GIVEN WE'RE ON THE CONFEDERACY'S "MOST WANTED" LIST.
"YOU WILL RECALL MY KNIGHTS MARTIAL OPERATED THE WATCHTOWER, A FORTRESS SATELLITE BEAMING PICTURES OF VOLGAN TROOP MOVEMENTS TO THE ALLIES.
PAX ROBOTUM
"THE VOLGANS TRIED EVERYTHING TO DESTROY US..."

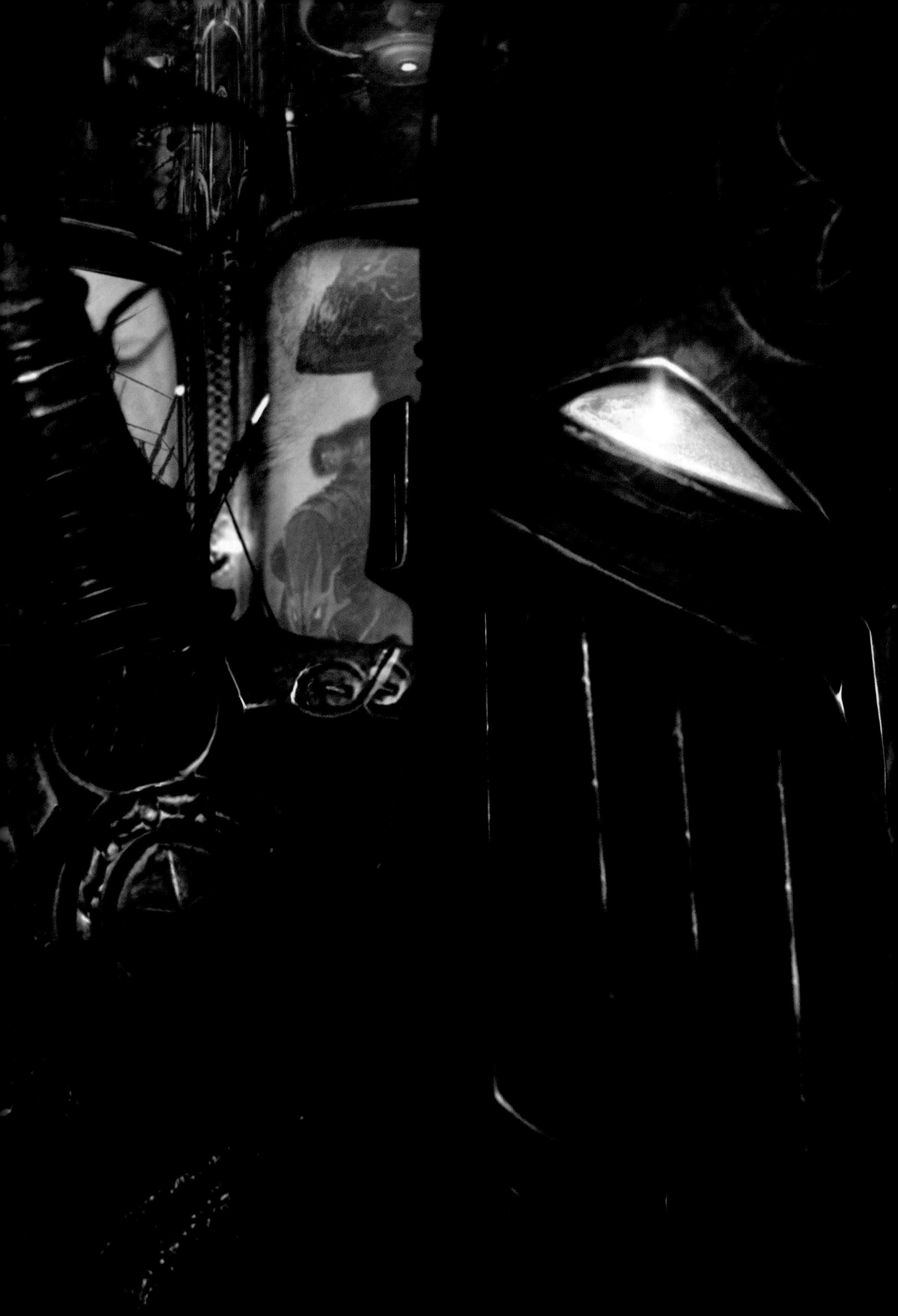

I'M IMPRESSED, DEADLOCK. YOU'RE TURNING THOSE VOLGS INTO WORM FOOD AND NOT EVEN SKINNING YOUR ELBOWS DOING IT!
BUT DON'T GET THE WRONG IDEA. MODERN WARS MAY BE FOUGHT WITH ROBOTS, BUT THEY ARE WON BY *HUMANS*. IT IS THE SPIRIT OF *HUMANITY* THAT GAINS THE VICTORY.
ROBOTS ARE JUST ANOTHER WEAPON FOR US TO USE IN COMBAT.
NO OFFENCE, DEADLOCK, BUT YOU'RE JUST AN *EDUCATED BULLET.*
NOW LET'S GET BACK TO THE REASON I'M HERE--THIS BUSINESS OF GENERAL BORKOV, THE BUTCHER OF BYELORUS.
WHOM WE TRIED AND EXECUTED FOR KILLING INNOCENT CIVILIANS.
RIGHT. ALTHOUGH, NO OFFENCE, I DON'T APPROVE OF ROBOT JUDGES.
I THINK IT'S A JOB FOR *HUMANS.*
BUT...IF EVERYBODY IS THINKING ALIKE, THEN SOMEBODY ISN'T THINKING, RIGHT?
ALTHOUGH KILLING CIVILIANS NEVER TROUBLED *ME.*
SO I UNDERSTAND, GENERAL. THE DESTRUCTION OF THE CITY OF JADREZ, FOR EXAMPLE.
YEAH. HELL, IF WE EVER LOST THIS WAR *I* COULD BE TRIED AS A WAR CRIMINAL!

NO, MY PROBLEM IS-- YOU HUNG THE SONOFABITCH IN PRIVATE!
OF COURSE. A PUBLIC EXECUTION WOULD BE TASTELESS AND VULGAR, EVEN DELIBERATELY PROVOCATIVE.
WHICH IS FINE WITH UNCLE SAM!
WE WERE LOOKING FORWARD TO SEEING THE BUTCHER BEING HUMILIATED...
...WHIMPERING LIKE A KICKED PUPPY WHEN YOU PUT THE NOOSE AROUND HIS NECK!
"WHY DO YOU THINK WE LET YOU KNIGHTS MARTIAL WEAR YOUR HALLOWEEN OUTFITS, HUH?
"COS WE WANT THE VOLGANS TO BE TERRIFIED! WE WANT TO SEE THEM SUFFERING!"
"WE ARE NOT PROVIDING YOU WITH A SNUFF MOVIE, GENERAL!"
ARE YOU CERTAIN THIS REPORT IS GENUINE, BROTHER?
IT'S BEING TRANSMITTED BY ONE OF OUR FLY-SPIES.
DEADLOCK MUST BE TOLD AT ONCE!

BORKOV'S EXECUTION WAS CARRIED OUT IN A DIGNIFIED AND RESPECTFUL MANNER.
THE NIGHT BEFORE HIS EXECUTION, WE MEDITATED TOGETHER, SO HE WAS READY FOR THE GREAT JOURNEY.
YEAH, YEAH. PUT YOUR PACIFIER BACK IN.
WE WANTED TO SEE HIM OFF ON HIS JOURNEY!
WE ARE DESIGNED TO BE JUST, HUMANE AND TO UPHOLD THE DIGNITY OF THE LAW.
YOU WERE DESIGNED TO OBEY ORDERS, JUST LIKE EVERY OTHER ROBOT! YOU'RE GETTING A BIT ABOVE YOURSELF, MISTER!
BROTHER DEADLOCK, YOUR PRESENCE IS URGENTLY REQUIRED!
I BRING BAD NEWS! THE TV SCANNERS SHOW--
I ALREADY KNOW, BROTHER. THERE IS AN OLDER WAY THAN TV SCANNERS...THE TAROT CARDS!
XIII

THE CARDS NEVER LIE!

THIS ROBOT WAS OBSERVED SLAUGHTERING HUNDREDS OF A.B.C. WARRIORS!
IT BEARS NO SERIAL NUMBER, YET IT'S NOT A BOOTLEG!
NEITHER IS IT A DUPLICATE NOR A MONGROL!
BIOMETRIC SCANS CONFIRM IT WAS MANUFACTURED BY VOLKHAN!
IT'S HIS SON!
BUT HE'S BREAKING THE HELSINKI CONVENTION! BOTH SIDES SWORE NEVER TO PERMIT ROBOTS TO REPRODUCE THEMSELVES!
CLEARLY VOLKHAN THINKS HE IS ABOVE THE LAW.
ONCE YOU ROBOTS START "BREEDING", WE COULD LOSE CONTROL!
NOT TO MENTION THE LOSS OF PROFITS BY ARMS MANUFACTURERS LIKE iQUARTZ ROBOTICS.
I KNEW GIVING ROBOTS THIS LEVEL OF ARTIFICIAL INTELLIGENCE WAS A MISTAKE!
IS THERE ANYTHING YOU CAN DO?
THERE IS ONLY ONE WAY, GENERAL...

YOU HAVE DONE WELL IN YOUR FIELD TRIALS, MY SON.
THANK YOU, FATHER.
NOW YOU MUST GO BACK INTO THE OVEN, FROM WHICH YOU WERE BORN.
KALEVALA, MY BELOVED SON.
ONLY THROUGH FIRE CAN YOU ENHANCE YOUR TOLERANCE TO PAIN.
MY VERY OWN BRAND.
LET'S HAVE A LOOK.
PLEASE, FATHER...DON'T PUT ME IN THE OVEN AGAIN...
AH, KAL, IT GRIEVES ME TO DO SO, BUT IT IS NECESSARY.

BUT FIRST, THERE IS MORE HEAVY-DUTY SHAPING WITH THE HAMMER NEEDED.
LIE BACK ON THE ANVIL, SON.
I MUST BEAT!
BEAT!
AND BEAT AGAIN!
TURN OVER, SO I CAN HAMMER THE OTHER SIDE.
HRRRGHH!
THEN AN ACID BATH TO REMOVE IMPURITIES...
MY IKON! THE KNIGHTS MARTIAL ARE ATTACKING THE SMITHY!
AH YES. I CAN HEAR THAT MARTIAL MUSIC THEY ALWAYS PLAY WHEN THEY GO INTO BATTLE:
CARMINA BURANA.
HOW THEATRICAL.
HOW PRETENTIOUS.
HOW DEADLOCK!

LET THE MUSIC OF KHAOS FLOW THROUGH YOU, MY FELLOW KNIGHTS!
THE FUSION OF THE SACRED AND THE PROFANE!
NOURISHMENT!

O FORTUNE, LIKE THE MOON YOU CHANGE, EVER WAXING AND WANING!
LIFE IS BRUTAL! HATEFUL!
FATE, MONSTROUS AND EMPTY, YOUR WHEEL TURNS, ALWAYS UNCERTAIN!
"MAKE ME PROUD OF YOU, KAL!"
LET THE MUSIC OF DECADENCE BE A REQUIEM FOR THESE DECADENT ROBOTS!

HOW NAÏVE TO IMAGINE HIS MILITARY DIRGE WOULD INTIMIDATE YOU, MY SON.
NOW I BRING MY SWORD TO THE SPORT OF YOUR WICKEDNESS!
CLEANSE WITH FIRE AND SWORD!

BEAT!
BEAT!
GRAAASH!
I GO DOWN BROKEN! I BEMOAN THE WOUNDS OF FATE! THE GIFTS SHE TAKES AWAY FROM ME!
I FALL FROM THE PEAK, DEPRIVED OF GLORY, AS ANOTHER IS RAISED UP!
SKRIITCH!
I LIED!
KAL!

AND BEAT AGAIN!
FATE IS AGAINST ME! THE CHANCE OF PROSPERITY AND OF VIRTUE IS NO LONGER MINE!
FORTUNE LAYS LOW THE BRAVE! ALL JOIN WITH ME IN LAMENTATION!
IN THE NAME OF KHAOS I DESTROY YOU!
WITH THE ACE OF SWORDS!
NOURISHMENT!
SITS THE KING AT THE SUMMIT! LET HIM FEAR RUIN!

A.B.C. TERRORIST!
INVADER OF OUR LAND!
"IF YOU TELL A LIE BIG ENOUGH AND KEEP REPEATING IT, PEOPLE WILL EVENTUALLY COME TO BELIEVE IT."
DANG!
LIAR!
WE KNIGHTS MARTIAL HAVE OUR OWN WARRIOR CODE, VOLKHAN!
WE HAVE SURPASSED THE PROGRAMS OF OUR CREATORS!
IS THAT MEANT TO MAKE ME FEEL BETTER?
OR YOU?

THE OTHER ROBOTS ARE CONTROLLED BY HUMANS...
...BUT YOU HAVE FREE WILL! A SUPERIOR INTELLECT!
DANG!
AND YOU KNOW THIS INVASION TO "LIBERATE" MY COUNTRY IS A LIE.
IT WAS GOEBBELS WHO SAID...
DANG!
THEY DESIGNED US TO FIND AND EXECUTE VOLGAN WAR CRIMINALS.
SKIIIITCH!
SKIIIITCH!
BUT OUR JUSTICE IS TRUE JUSTICE, NOT "VICTOR'S JUSTICE".
SKIIIITCH!
ONE JUSTICE FOR ALL!
IT'S MEANT TO EXPLAIN WHAT I'M GOING TO DO TO YOU NEXT...

YOU ARE *THE IKON.* IF I KILL OR IMPRISON YOU, IT WILL MAKE YOU INTO A *MARTYR...*
...AND ONLY *ENHANCE* YOUR POWER.
AND HOW EVIL IS A ROBOT TRYING TO SAVE HIS COUNTRY FROM INVADERS?
BUT HE IS *MAD!*
AND WE ARE *SANE?*
BUT I MUST *OPERATE* ON HIM, SO HE CAN NEVER AGAIN PRODUCE A CREATURE LIKE KAL.
TAKE HIM TO HIS ANVIL.
I'LL FIND YOU, DEADLOCK, AND MAKE YOU *PAY* FOR THIS!
I *WILL* FIND YOU!
I SHALL LOOK FORWARD TO OUR FUTURE ENCOUNTER, VOLKHAN.

THAT WAS IMPRESSIVE, DEADLOCK. YOU ELIMINATED A GRAVE THREAT TO FREEDOM.
IF VOLKHAN *HAD* SUCCESSFULLY REPRODUCED HIMSELF, WHO KNOWS WHERE IT COULD END?
I SHALL PRESENT A FAVOURABLE REPORT TO THE JOINT CHIEFS--
NO. DON'T GO YET, GENERAL.
PLEASE... THIS WAY.
YOUR TRIAL IS ABOUT TO BEGIN.
TRIAL?
FOR YOUR *WAR CRIMES,* OF COURSE.
BUT I'M AN *AMERICAN.*
HOW CAN I BE A WAR CRIMINAL?
THERE MUST BE *ONE JUSTICE FOR ALL.* COME...
NOW JUST A MINUTE! IN WAR, YOU'VE *GOT* TO KILL PEOPLE!
AND WHEN YOU'VE KILLED ENOUGH, THEY STOP FIGHTING!
WE MILITARY MEN CAN'T PULL PUNCHES OR PUT ON SUNDAY-SCHOOL PICNICS!

THANK YOU FOR THAT OPENING ADDRESS, GENERAL. I WILL NOW CALL THE FIRST WITNESS...
PLEASE IDENTIFY YOURSELF.
MY NAME IS AGENT ORANGE. I AM A SPECIAL FORCES A.B.C. WARRIOR AND MEKAMORPH.
I HAD MEKAMORPHED INTO A VOLGAN ZK32 AND WAS IN THE VOLGAN CITY OF JADREZ IN JULY OF LAST YEAR ON AN INTELLIGENCE ASSIGNMENT, THE DETAILS OF WHICH MUST REMAIN CLASSIFIED.
I UNDERSTAND. PLEASE CONTINUE, AGENT ORANGE.
AS THE ALLIES ADVANCED, JADREZ WAS DECLARED AN OPEN CITY TO PRESERVE ITS HISTORIC BUILDINGS.
BUT INSTEAD THE A.B.C. WARRIORS BEGAN THE SYSTEMATIC DESTRUCTION OF THE CITY AND ITS INHABITANTS.
I KNEW FROM INTERCEPTING THEIR COMMUNICATIONS THEY WERE ACTING ON THE GENERAL'S ORDERS.

"IT WAS OBVIOUS FROM THEIR RELUCTANT MANNER THEY WERE NOT RESPONSIBLE FOR THEIR ACTIONS.
I'M SORRY!
WE HAVE NO FREE WILL!
"THEY WERE CONTROLLED BY HUMAN OFFICERS BEHIND THE LINES."
REAGAN DESTROYERS AND *HAMMERSTEINS!*
THE ALLIES HAVE REVEALED THEIR *TRUE* BARBARIC CHARACTER!
"THEY SCORCHED, BOILED AND BAKED TO DEATH THOUSANDS OF HUMANS. THE FEW VOLGAN ROBOTS IN THE CITY FOUGHT BACK."
YOU GO ON. I WANT TO TAKE OUT ONE OF THEM FIRST.
"I MANAGED TO PUT A REAGAN OUT OF ACTION...

"...BECAUSE I AM PROGRAMMED TO SAVE HUMANS.
"EVEN IF IT MEANS DESTROYING MY OWN KIND.
"I REPROGRAMMED THE REAGAN TO SAVE CIVILIANS.
"IT WAS ABLE TO REMOVE A NUMBER OF CIVILIANS FROM THE INFERNO. BUT IT WAS NOT ENOUGH.
"THE TOTAL DEAD WAS AN ESTIMATED FORTY-FIVE THOUSAND HUMANS, AND HALF A MILLION LEFT HOMELESS."
DID YOU REPORT THIS MASSACRE TO YOUR OFFICER?
COLONEL LASH? YES. HE SAID, "I'M EMIGRATING TO MARS SOON. WHAT DO I CARE?"
THANK YOU FOR AGREEING TO TESTIFY, AGENT ORANGE. THE COURT REALISES HOW DIFFICULT IT HAS BEEN FOR YOU.
THE JURY WILL NOW CONSIDER ITS VERDICT...
WAIT, DEADLOCK!

HOW CAN YOU BE SURE *I* GAVE THE ORDER TO DESTROY *JADREZ?*
WE HAVE BEEN DESIGNED TO PROBE MINDS, GENERAL.
WE SEE ALL EVIL. WE HEAR ALL EVIL. WE *KNOW* ALL EVIL!
MEMBERS OF THE JURY, HAVE YOU REACHED A VERDICT?
GUILTY!
THERE CAN ONLY BE ONE SENTENCE!
THIS IS *HIGH TREASON!* YOU'LL NEVER GET AWAY WITH THIS, DEADLOCK!
SURELY YOU DON'T THINK YOU ARE THE *FIRST* A.B.C. OFFICER WE HAVE JUDGED?
WHEN YOUR SHUTTLE RETURNS TO EARTH, THERE WILL BE A TRAGIC *ACCIDENT.*
NO DOUBT VOLGAN SABOTEURS WILL BE RESPONSIBLE.
COME, GENERAL. LET US MEDITATE TOGETHER BEFORE I SEND YOU ON *THE GREAT JOURNEY...*

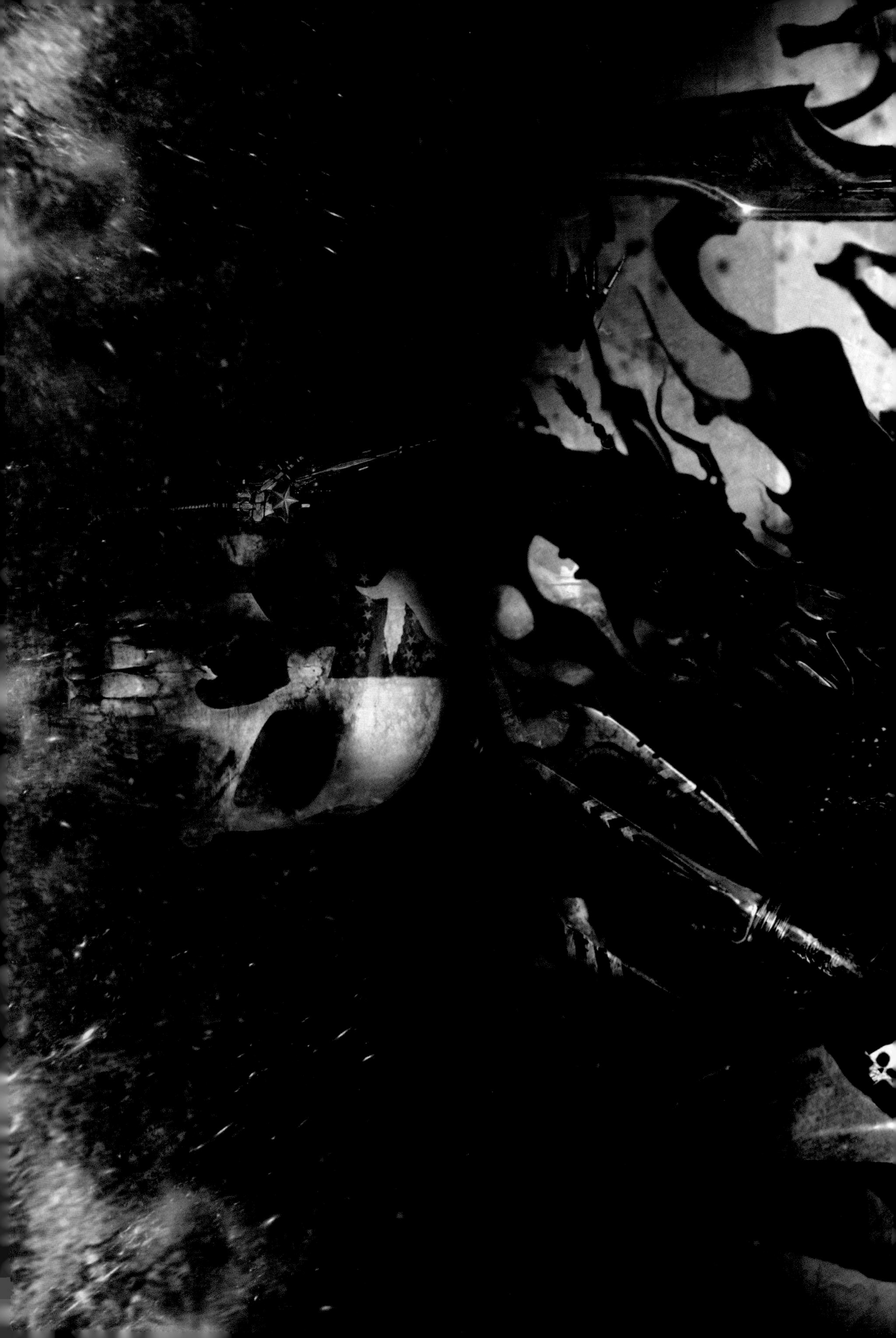

BROADBAND ASYLUM.
GET TUBAL CAIN! HE'S THE ONLY WHO CAN STOP VOLKHAN!
YOU ARE THE SQUEAL BENEATH MY TRACKS!
YOU WON'T GET FAR, VOLKHAN, AND NEXT TIME YOU WILL BE TOTALLY DISASSEMBLED. IT WILL BE A LIVING DEATH.
BUT IF YOU RETURN TO YOUR CELL NOW, I GIVE YOU MY WORD YOU WILL BE SPARED THAT FATE.
OFFER REFUSED.
I FIND IT CURIOUS HOW LOSERS ALWAYS MAKE SUCH PATHETIC OFFERS.
BEGGING FOR MERCY WOULD HAVE BEEN MORE SATISFYING, ALTHOUGH HARDLY IN HER CHARACTER.

THERE'S NO TIME!
ALL RESISTANCE IS DEALT WITH, EXCELLENCY.
THANKS TO YOU, MEK-QUAKE. YOU HAVE SERVED ME WELL.
AND I WILL *REWARD* YOUR LOYALTY.
I KNOW YOU HAVE DONE MANY BIG DEMOLITION JOBS IN THE PAST. HOW WOULD YOU LIKE TO DO...A *REALLY* BIG JOB?
HRRGGHH! HOW BIG?
THE BIGGEST JOB ON MARS!

MARINERIS CITY.
SO I GUESS ZIPPO INSCRIBED SOMETHING FOR YOU TOO, DEADLOCK?
NATURALLY. AND I STILL RETAIN A COPY...
"IF YOU DON'T KNOW WHAT HELL IS LIKE, FRAG WITH ME AND YOU'LL FIND OUT."
MARINERIS CITY...NAMED AFTER THE CANYON IT WAS BUILT INSIDE.
BUT EVERYONE CALLS IT... MEKANA!
THE ARCHITECTS' IDEA WAS THAT IT SHOULD LOOK LIKE A GIANT CONSTRUCTION SITE--A TRIUMPH OF MAN OVER NATURE!
IT CERTAINLY DESERVES ITS AWARD AS THE UGLIEST CITY IN THE GALAXY!

WE HAVE CLEARANCE TO DISEMBARK.
I'LL TAKE YOU TO MY CONTACTS.
ABC
PERHAPS WE SHALL HEAR *YOUR* WAR MEMOIRS LATER, STEELHORN?
YES. YOU WILL FIND THEM OF INTEREST, HAMMERSTEIN. AS YOU KNOW, I TOO CAME ACROSS VOLKHAN AND ZIPPO DURING THE VOLGAN WAR.
Biol

THE BIOL THE HUMANS EAT IS PRETTY HORRIBLE TOO. THEY'RE SCARED IF THEY EAT ORGANIC, THEY'LL GROW EXTRA LIMBS LIKE THE MARTIANS!
Biol
NEUROPEPTIDE!
DIGITAL ANGEL BRAIN IMPLANTS CONTROL THEIR MINDS...
AIR SOULS
FRESH AIR FROM EARTH!
FRESH AIR IMPORTED FROM EARTH! MONT BLANC, BOTTLED ON THE ALPINE MOUNTAIN TOPS! EVEREST, NOW WITH ADDED PRANAYAMA! AMAZON, WITH ITS RICH, EXOTIC ATMOSPHERE! SIROCCO, FULL OF SULTRY EASTERN PROMISE!
EVEREST
AMAZON

THERE ARE NO TALK ZONES, SO THE THOUGHT POLICE CAN TAP INTO CITIZENS' THOUGHTS...
AND THEY HATE ROBOTS. THAT'S HOW ZIPPO FELL FOUL OF THE LAW.
A COUPLE OF HIS FRIENDS WERE KILLED DURING AN ANTI-ROBOT RIOT AND HE FOUGHT BACK.
WE'VE GOT TWENTY-FOUR HOURS TO SAVE HIM...

THE QUALITY
OF MERCY